The Mermaid Princess

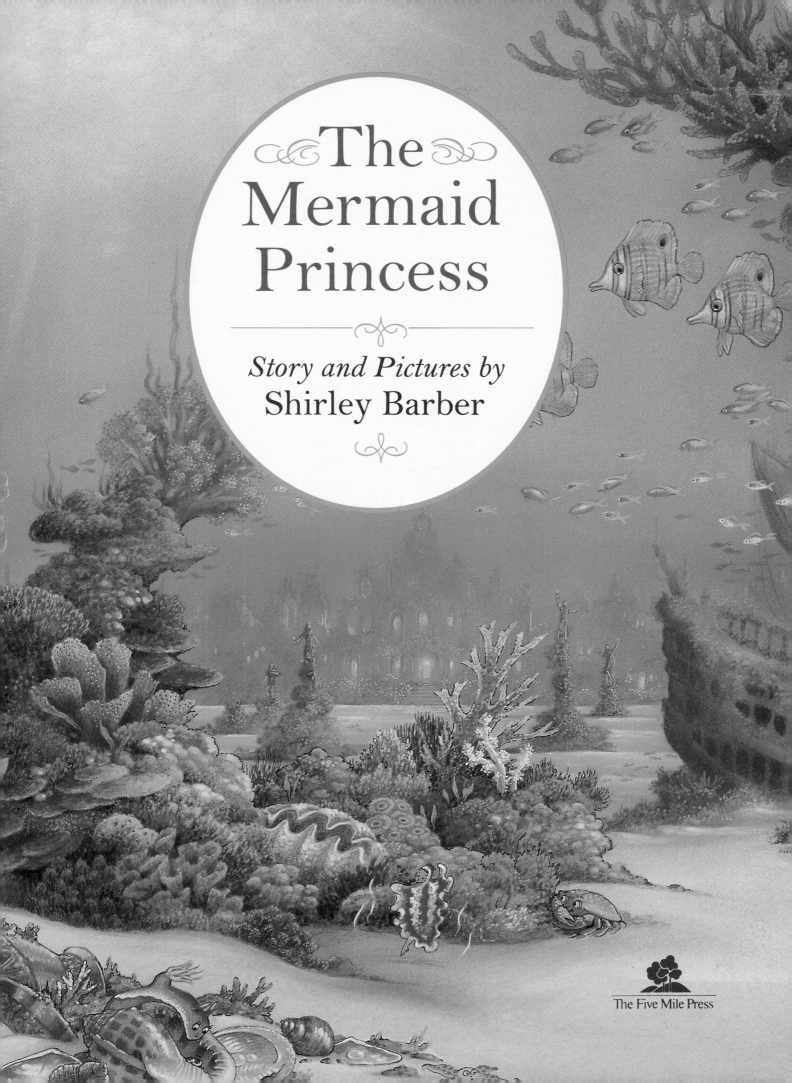

The Mermaid Princess

Story and Pictures by
Shirley Barber

The Five Mile Press

In a tropical ocean lay a small green island surrounded by sandy beaches and a coral reef. At high tide, when the sea covered the reef, it flowered like a magical garden — filled with brilliant fish, swaying plants and strange sea creatures. There was only one house on the island and in it lived two children, Jon and Wendy, and their father and mother.

It was holiday time. The children's father spent all day in his boat fishing, and their mother was busy writing a book. Wendy was recovering from the flu, and still felt rather weak. She just lay on a couch gazing out to sea, or down into a big coral pool not far from her window. Nothing seemed to interest her.

Jon liked to wander over the reef at low tide. When he found something really unusual he would bring it inside to show Wendy. What he didn't realise was that he was being watched all the while by somebody very small hidden amongst the coral. It was Sandy the seashore pixie. Sandy lived in a sandcastle decorated with bits of green and white sea-smoothed glass.

Early each morning, Sandy pushed his little cart along the tideline to see what had been washed up. He found beanpods and shells which he used to keep things in, and sticks for his fire. But what he liked to find most of all were pieces of coloured glass. He always hoped to find really colourful ones, of sparkling red or blue, but somehow he never did.

One morning, Sandy was amazed to find a beautiful mermaid sitting among the coral, frightened and sad. She told Sandy that her name was Marina.

Marina said she had been riding with her friends on their dolphins, a long way from the underwater city where they lived. Suddenly a huge shark had charged them, scattering the dolphins. Marina on her white dolphin, Silverfin, had sped away pursued by the shark. In a terrifying chase Silverfin had tried to outswim the shark.

In desperation, Silverfin tossed Marina out of the water, so that he could swim faster. Then he led the shark away.

"I cut my tail on the sharp coral," Marina tearfully told the pixie. "So now I can't swim home. Poor Silverfin might have been killed, and the shark is probably waiting in the deep water to catch me too. Whatever shall I do?"

Sandy didn't know what to say. He knew that when the tide returned it would sweep the mermaid over the sharp coral and she would be hurt again. Just then Jon appeared over the reef. Sandy quickly hid. To the little pixie, Jon was as big as a giant.

"A real mermaid!" exclaimed Jon. "I've just got to show her to Wendy!" He carefully picked up Marina and carried her back to the coral pool near his sister's window.

Jon ran inside the house. "Wendy," he gasped. "I've found a real-live mermaid! I've put her in your coral pool so you can see her through your window."

His sister sat up and looked out at the pool. Sure enough, there was the mermaid. She was calmly tidying her golden hair. At last something *did* interest Wendy! "Isn't she beautiful!" she cried.

"Yes, but we must keep her a secret," said Jon, "or she might be taken away and put in an aquarium."

That night, when the moon had risen high in the sky, Wendy awoke with a start. She looked out of the window. Yes, the mermaid was still there — and she was talking to a tiny figure! Wendy got up rather shakily and tiptoed to wake Jon. Together they slipped out of the house and down to the coral pool.

At first the mermaid and the pixie were too shy to answer Jon and Wendy's eager questions.

"*Please* talk to us," Wendy begged. "We only want to help you." So Sandy introduced himself and Marina to the children. Then Marina told them her story.

"Somehow we must tell Marina's people where she is so that they can come and fetch her," said Jon, when she had finished. "I could go," offered Sandy, "I have a boat."

"I could anchor it at the edge of the reef," Sandy added. "Then I could dive down and look for the underwater city."

"But how will you breathe under water?" Jon asked.

"Seashore pixies can breathe under water as well as on land," Sandy replied.

Marina said he would need a snack for the journey, and gave him some dainty kelp biscuits.

Sandy sailed out over the reef and anchored where
the deep water began. He bravely let himself sink down,
down through the dark water till he landed on the
sea-floor. With each surge of the sea he could hear a
bell softly chiming. He could just see faint lights
glimmering in the distance. Sandy felt sure it must
be the underwater city so he set off over the sand
towards it.

He walked all night. When the sun rose, a soft radiance lit the underwater world. Now Sandy saw huge wrecked ships on the sea-floor, and he passed treasure chests, broken open and spilling jewels onto the sand. To Sandy they looked like the prettiest bits of coloured glass he'd ever seen. But he felt he shouldn't pick them up without asking the merpeople first.

At last he could see the underwater city quite clearly. He was almost at the end of his journey.

Suddenly shoals of fish sped past him in fright. They called out to Sandy as they passed, "Hide quickly! Here comes the shark! He'll eat you up for his lunch."

Sandy crept into an empty clam shell and hoped the huge shark would not notice him as it circled above.

But the shark quickly spied the little pixie inside the clam shell. "Come out and let me look at you," he snarled. "You'll have to come out sooner or later — and I'm very patient," he added with a horrible smile.

Poor Sandy felt very frightened.

Sandy suddenly realised he was starving. Then he remembered Marina's biscuits which he ate straight away. After a while he began to feel hungry again — but still the shark circled above. Suddenly, a gleaming white dolphin came flashing through the water. It was Silverfin, who made straight for the shark, followed by many other dolphins.

The huge shark decided there were too many for him to fight, so he sped away. Sandy crept out of his clam shell and gratefully climbed onto Silverfin's back. Then Silverfin carried him swiftly towards the city of the merpeople.

The merpeople gathered around Sandy. When he had told his story they set before him a lovely meal of sea-fruit and coral cakes.

Sandy discovered that Marina was a mermaid princess, the youngest daughter of the mer-king. Her brothers and sisters were eager to rescue her, but the king said, "We must all go together. The shark will be afraid to attack so many of us."

So the merpeople mounted their dolphins and Silverfin led the way, carrying Sandy.

They swam to the edge of the reef which rose like a cliff before them. Silverfin carried Sandy up to his little boat and helped him climb in. The tide was not high enough for the dolphins and the merpeople to swim safely over the sharp pointed coral. So they waited in the deep water while Sandy carefully steered his little boat between the jagged pieces of coral towards the shore.

When the boat touched the sand the pixie jumped out and ran to the coral pool. Marina was overjoyed to see he was safe. He told the little mermaid that her family was waiting for her beyond the reef.

"But how can I reach them?" she cried. "The coral is so sharp!"

Just then Jon and Wendy came running down. They had seen Sandy returning in his boat. When they had heard his news Jon said, "I'll carry Marina out to where the water is deep enough for her to swim safely."

Wendy stood on the beach with Sandy and watched anxiously as Jon carried Marina out over the coral. At first he was paddling, then wading. At last, when the water was up to Jon's waist, Marina could see her people.

"Goodbye, Jon," she cried. "Thank you so much for all your help." Then she slipped from his arms. With a splash of her gleaming tail she was on her way.

Marina joyfully greeted her beloved dolphin Silverfin and was soon surrounded by her family and friends. It was a sight that Jon and Wendy would never forget.

andy slipped away to hide. The children seemed very big to him, and he was still a little afraid of them.

Next morning when he pushed his cart along the tideline as usual he found a thank-you gift from the merpeople.

It was a chest full of brightly-coloured jewels! So now Sandy's castle really sparkles in the sunshine — just as he had always dreamed it would.